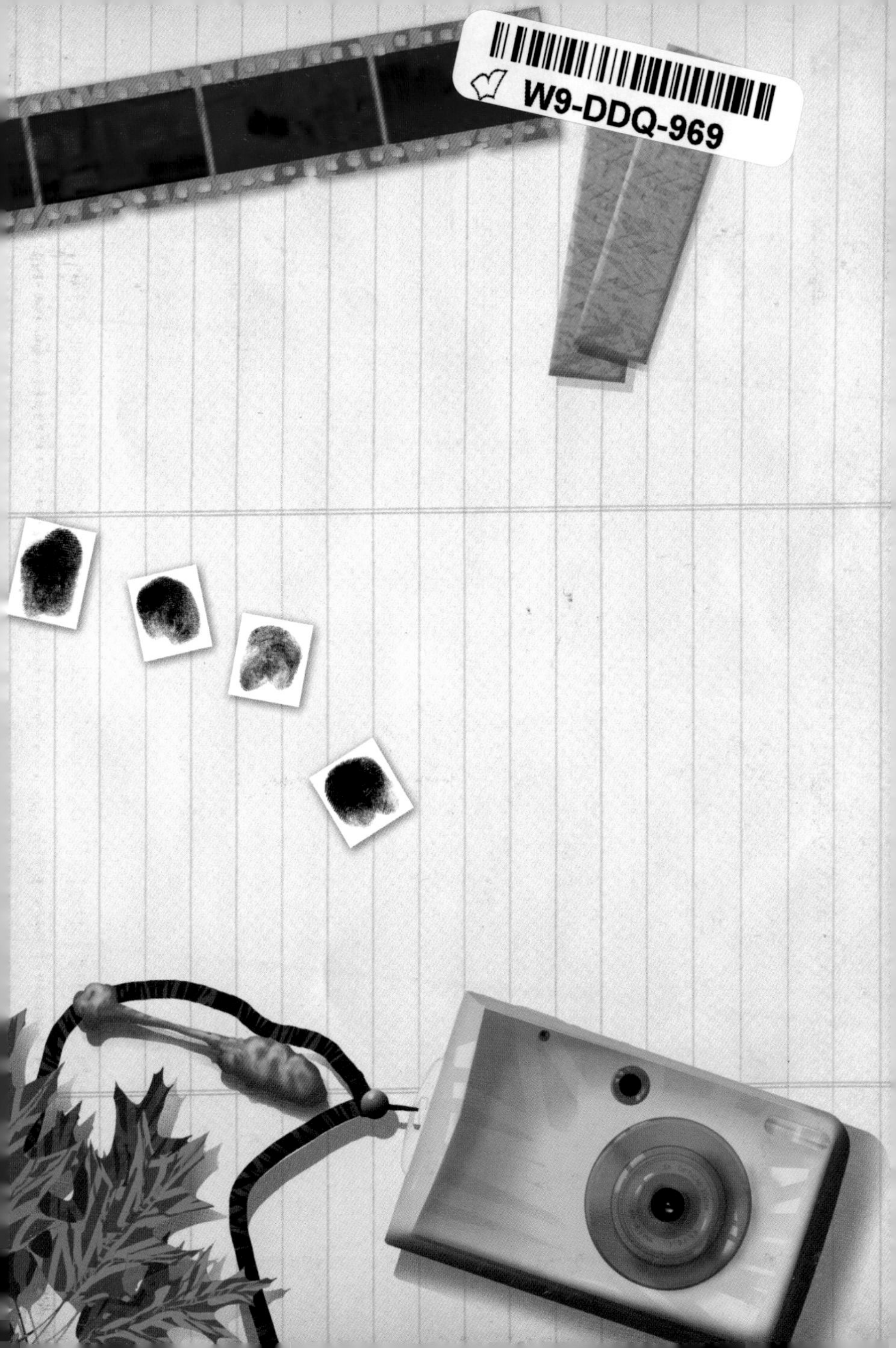

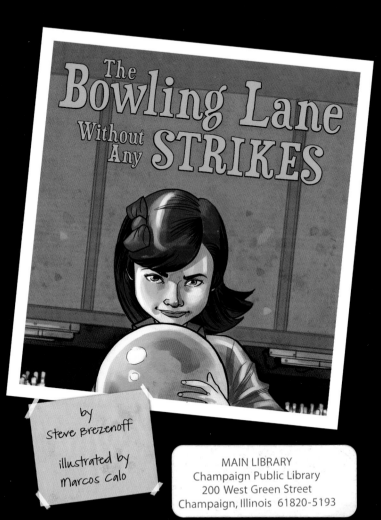

FIELD TRIP MYSTERIES

The Bowling Lane Without Any STRIKES

by
Steve Brezenoff

illustrated by
Marcos Calo

STONE ARCH BOOKS
a capstone imprint

r Samantha Archer,

Field Trip Mysteries are published by Stone Arch Books
A Capstone Imprint
1710 Roe Crest Drive
North Mankato, Minnesota 55603
www.capstonepub.com

Library of Congress Cataloging-in-Publication Data
Brezenoff, Steven.
   The bowling lane without any strikes / by Steve Brezenoff;
illustrated by Marcos Calo.
       p. cm. -- (Field trip mysteries)
   ISBN 978-1-4342-5979-0 (library binding)
   ISBN 978-1-4342-6212-7 (pbk.)
1. School field trips--Juvenile fiction. 2. Bowling--Juvenile
fiction. 3. Bowling alleys--Juvenile fiction. 4. Sabotage--
Juvenile fiction. [1. Mystery and detective stories. 2. School
field trips--Fiction. 3. Bowling--Fiction. 4. Bowling alleys-
-Fiction. 5. Sabotage--Fiction.] I. Calo, Marcos, ill. II.
Title. III. Series: Brezenoff, Steven. Field trip mysteries.
PZ7.B7576Bow 2013   2012049377
   813.6--dc23

Graphic Designer: Kristi Carlson

Summary: Catalina "Cat" Duran and her sixth-grade class are on a bowling trip, but in one lane the ball keeps going mysteriously off track, so the four friends decide to investigate the problem.

Printed in China.
032013   007228RRDF13

TABLE OF CONTENTS

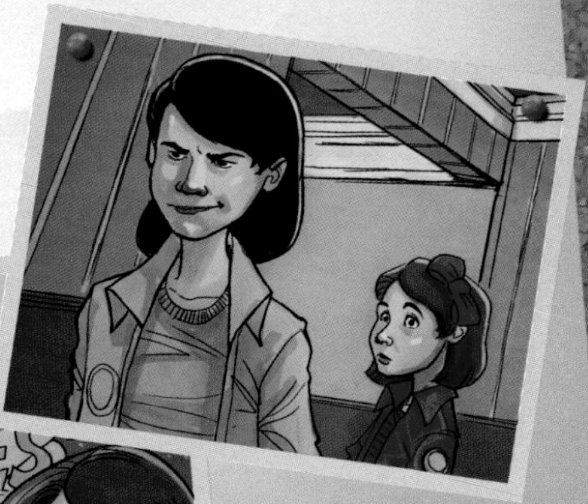

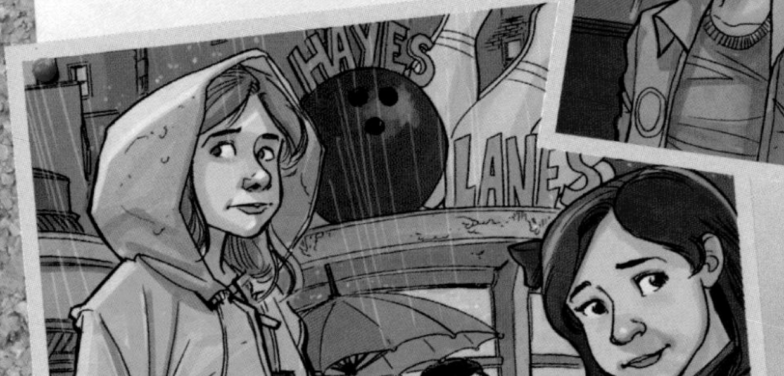
HAYES
LANES

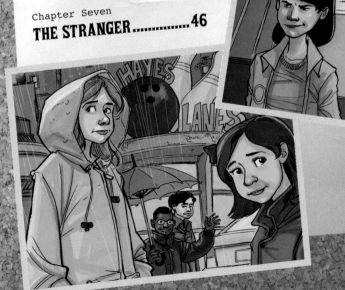

Catalina Duran

A.K.A: Cat

D.O.B: February 15th

POSITION: 6th Grade

INTERESTS:

Animals, being "green", field trips

KNOWN ASSOCIATES:

Archer, Samantha; Garrison, Edward; and Shoo, James. *Are these students spending too much time together?*

NOTES:

Catalina is well liked by most of her teachers and fellow students. *Sounds like a troublemaker.*

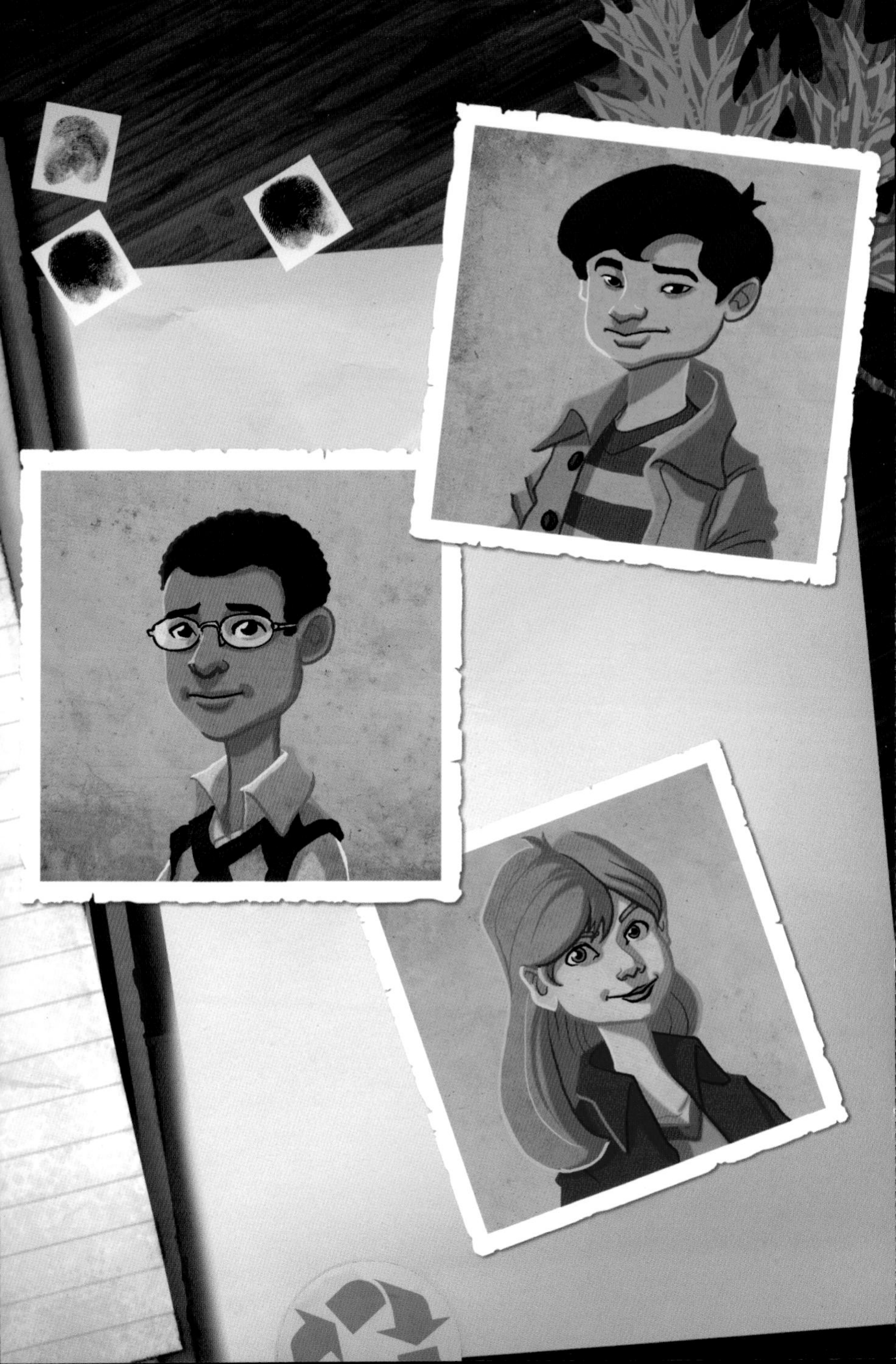

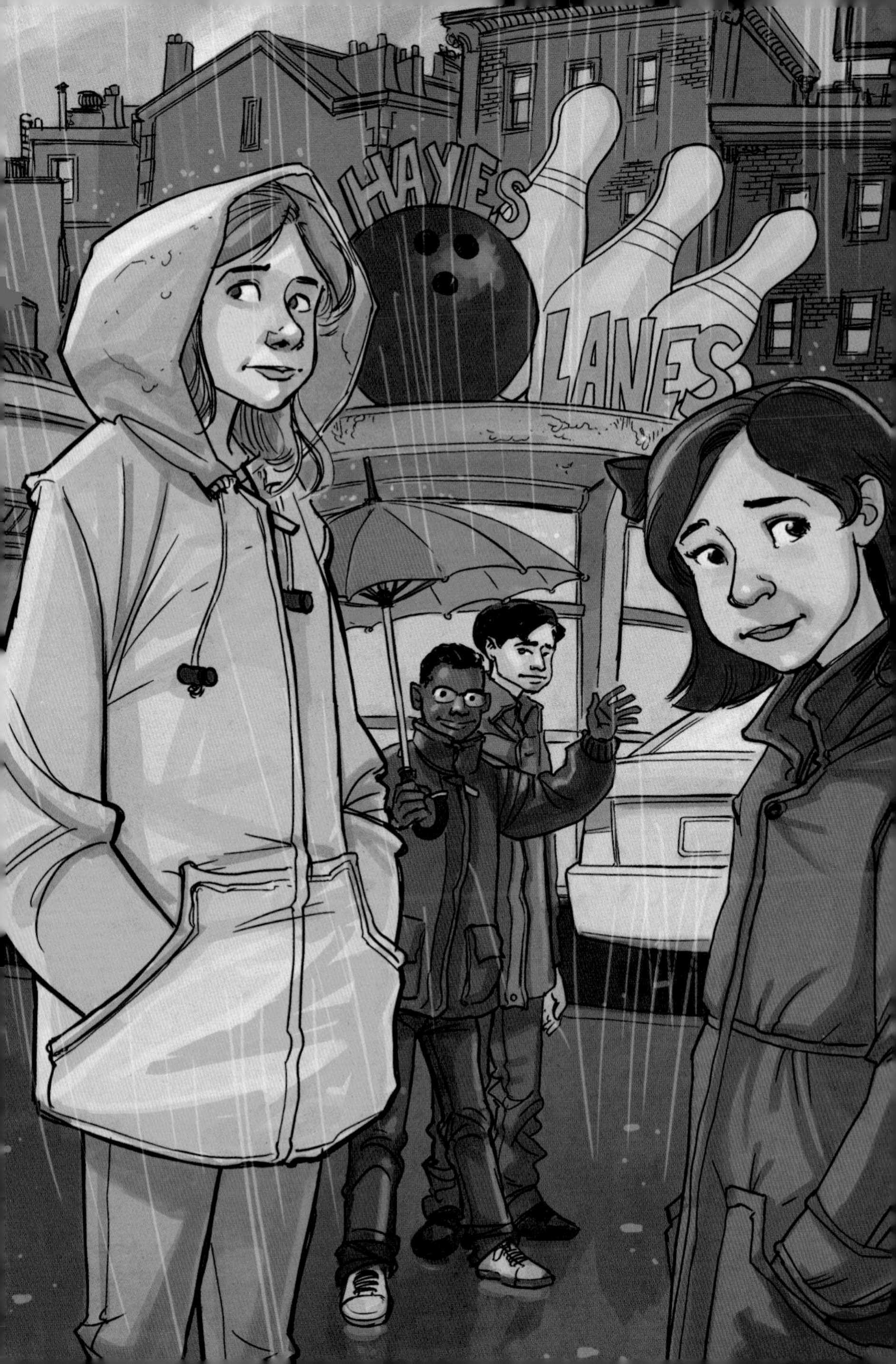
HAYES
LANES

CHAPTER ONE

BOWLING CHAMP

It was pouring on Monday morning, but that couldn't get me down. Mr. Spade's sixth-grade class huddled together and hurried across the wide sidewalk in front of the Two Rivers Bowling Alley.

Sam Archer, my best friend, pulled off her bright-yellow slicker and shook it out on the big mat. "Will this rain ever stop?" she asked.

"Yeah, three days of rain is more than enough," said Egg — that's what we call our friend Edward. He folded his umbrella and leaned it against the wall next to the door.

"Look on the bright side," said Gum. He's the fourth member of our circle of friends. His real name is James, but everyone calls him Gum. "At least we get to change our shoes."

"That doesn't sound like a bright side at all," I said. That was the one thing I didn't like about bowling: the smelly shoes.

"Everyone line up," announced Mr. Spade. "Shoes time! I hope you all know your size."

The whole class got in line at the shoe counter — except one girl.

Lily McDonald was new to our class. She sat down at a bench near the lanes to watch some early-morning bowlers.

"Save my spot," I told Gum, and he nodded. I walked over to Lily.

"Lily, it's time to line up to get shoes," I said.

She was so focused on a man bowling at the middle lane that she didn't hear me. I tapped her shoulder and she jumped.

"Huh?" she said. "Oh, Catalina. Did you need something?"

I smiled at her. "We're supposed to line up for shoes now," I said. I thumbed over my shoulder at the rest of the class already at the counter. "And you can call me Cat," I added.

"Oh, I have my own shoes," she said. She patted the bag next to her on the bench.

"I always bring my own shoes," she added. "And my own ball."

"You have your own shoes and ball?" I asked. "You must be really good!"

She nodded. "Yeah," she said. "Actually, on Saturday my dad and I won the Father-Daughter Championship here."

"That's great," I said. "Maybe you can teach me to be a great bowler too."

Lily shrugged. "I don't know," she said. "It takes a lot of practice. I've been bowling since I was three."

"Well," I said, "I better get back in line so I can get some shoes and start practicing."

"What was that all about?" Gum asked. Egg and Sam leaned in to hear too.

"Lily is a bowling champ," I said. "She has all her own stuff, like shoes and a ball."

"She's on my team!" Gum said.

We got our shoes — mine were green and blue with orange polka dots — and then Mr. Spade announced the teams.

"Three to each team so we're evenly divided," he said. Then he pointed at each of us in little clusters. We watched anxiously, hoping we'd end up on teams together. Of course, our little group of friends is four people. Someone would be left on his or her own.

"Quick," Gum said. "Go grab Lily."

"Me?" I asked.

He gave me a little shove and nodded. "Hurry!" he said.

So I ran across the lobby, grabbed Lily by the hand, and said, "Come with me."

Lily grabbed her bag as she said, "Okay." She sure was confused. We got back to the group just in time.

"You three," Mr. Spade said. He pointed at me, Gum, and Lily. "Lane one."

"Yes," said Gum. He pumped his fist. "We are *so* going to win."

Lily smiled and blushed.

"And you three," Mr. Spade called out. He pointed at Sam and Egg and another kid behind Sam. "Lane two."

Egg and Sam high-fived. Then they turned around to see who the third kid was.

"Hello, dorks," the kid said.

It was Anton Gutman.

"You should go first, Lily," Egg said. He sat down at lane two to tie up his shoes. Lily already had hers on.

"Me?" Lily asked. She polished her bright yellow bowling ball with small soft cloth.

"Why not?" said Sam. "Cat tells us you're a champ. Show us what you got!"

"She's a champion bowler?" said Anton. "Yeah, right."

"Hush up, Gutman," said Gum. "She brought her own ball."

"No way!" Anton said, stamping his foot. "That's an unfair advantage. We should all get to use expensive, fancy balls like hers instead of these lame, old balls."

We rolled our eyes at him. Mr. Spade called over. "Relax, Mr. Gutman," he said. "It's just a friendly morning of bowling. And maybe a few lessons in physics!"

"Go ahead," I said, patting Lily on the shoulder.

"Well, okay," Lily said. "I might as well take a few warm-up throws while you all get your shoes on and find balls."

Lily held one hand over the vent at the ball return. Then she dusted her hands with a little pouch of powder. She picked up her ball and held it before her face in front of lane one. She kept her feet together as she looked down the lane at the pins.

Then she took a deep breath, walked forward, and, just as she reached the fault line, drew back the ball and flung it forward.

Anyone could tell she knew what she was doing. The ball sped down the right side of the lane. Then, before it reached the pins, it took a little hop and bounced into the gutter.

"Ha, ha!" said Anton, laughing. "Some champion!"

Lily was stunned. "That was weird," she said.

"No, it wasn't," Anton said. "You threw the ball right next to the gutter. "

She glared at him but didn't respond.

"Take another one," I said.

Lily laughed it off. "Right," she said. "My arm is probably jelly from this weekend." She watched the ball return. Then she grabbed it and took another throw.

It was exactly the same. The ball zoomed down the right side. Then it wobbled, hopped, and flew into the gutter.

"This isn't even funny anymore," Anton said. "It's just sad. I'm going to get a pretzel."

Lily covered her face with her hands and slumped into her seat.

"Maybe she was just bragging," Sam said. The four of us — Me, Sam, Gum, and Egg — stood together just outside lanes one and two. Anton wasn't back with his pretzel yet, so the game couldn't really start. He'd insisted on going first. Of course.

"You mean maybe she was lying?" I asked. It didn't seem likely to me.

"Who's lying?" asked Mr. Spade. I guess he'd overheard us. He came over and put his hands on his hips.

"Oh, no one," Egg said. He explained what had happened.

"Hmm," Mr. Spade said. He looked at Lily, still slumped in her chair. She sure seemed sad. "Well, most people don't own their own bowling ball and bowling shoes if they don't bowl a lot."

"But you should've seen it," Gum said. "She rolled the ball right near the gutter. Anton may be nasty, but he was right about that."

Mr. Spade chuckled. "Actually," he said, "that's how the professional bowlers do it."

"Really?" I asked.

"Sure," said Mr. Spade. "Come on. I'll show you." He led me and my friends to lane number five.

That was the lane Lily had been watching, I realized, while we all lined up for our shoes. A man in an open button-up shirt and tan pants was about to bowl.

"Shh," Mr. Spade said. "Just watch."

The man walked up and threw the ball just like Lily had. His ball zoomed down the right side of the lane, looking like it might slip into the gutter at any second. But then, just before it reached the pins, it suddenly cut left.

"Whoa!" Gum said as it happened.

The ball hit the pins with a loud crack, like thunder clapping. All the pins went down. It was a strike.

"How did he do that?" Egg asked.

Sam screwed up her face like she does when we're solving a mystery.

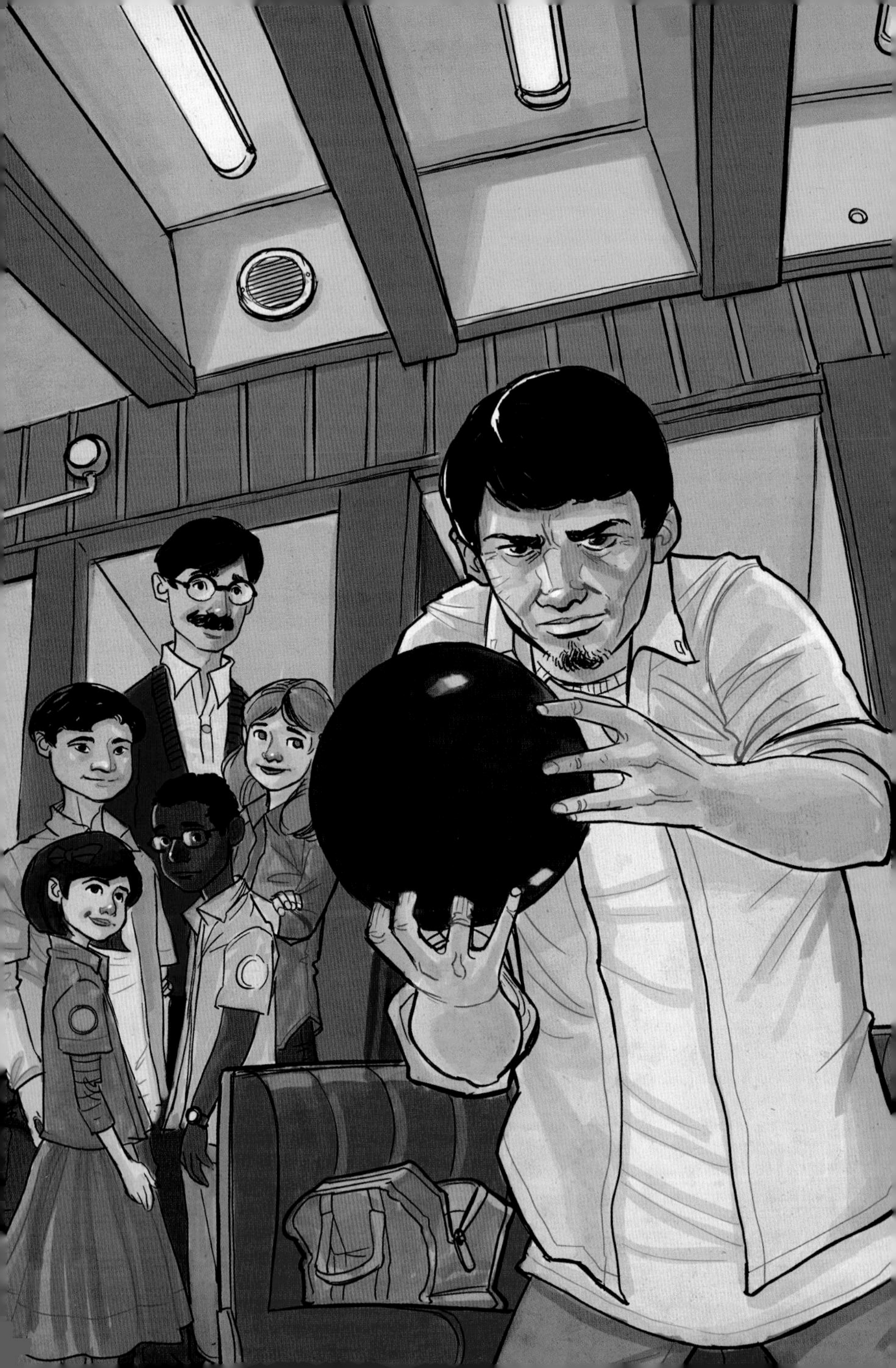

"See?" said Mr. Spade. "That bowler puts a lot of spin on the ball. Then, when the ball reaches the end of the lane, where it's not as slick, the spin makes it turn left very sharply."

"Wow," I said. "So Lily does know what she's doing."

Mr. Spade smiled. "It sure sounds like she does."

Back at lanes one and two, Anton was lounging with his feet up across the line of seats. Lily was sitting at lane one, as far away from him as possible, staring into space. She'd obviously been crying.

"There you dorks are," Anton said. "I went already. I got a spare."

"Really?" I said. "Nice job, Anton." I don't like Anton, but I try to be nice to him.

"I don't believe you," said Sam. She stomped right up to him.

Anton crossed his arms and sneered. "Well, it's true," he said. "Ask the champ over there." He nodded toward Lily.

"Well?" Gum said.

Lily nodded. "It's true," she said. "I got two gutter balls, and he got a spare."

"Those gutter balls didn't count," I said. I sat down next to her and patted her knee. "You were just warming up."

Anton laughed. "Not those," he said. "She already took her first real turn too. Two more gutter balls!" He laughed some more.

"That's okay," I told Lily. "Like you said, your arm is probably tired."

Lily gave me a smile, but it didn't look real.

"Well, I guess it's my turn," said Gum. He grabbed his ball, stepped up, and threw it down lane one.

The ball went pretty fast, but his aim was terrible. The ball bounced along with five great thuds before hitting two pins in the corner. "Two!" Gum shouted.

He didn't hit anything on his next throw, though. "Oh, well," he said. Then he sat down and popped a piece of gum into his mouth. It smelled like cherry cola.

"My turn," said Sam.

"Don't blow it, beanpole," said Anton. He crossed his arms.

Sam sneered at him and grabbed her ball. "I'm terrible," she said. "So don't expect much."

She stepped up to lane two. Then she drew her arm back, swung it forward, and released the ball. It bounced twice and headed straight to the head pin.

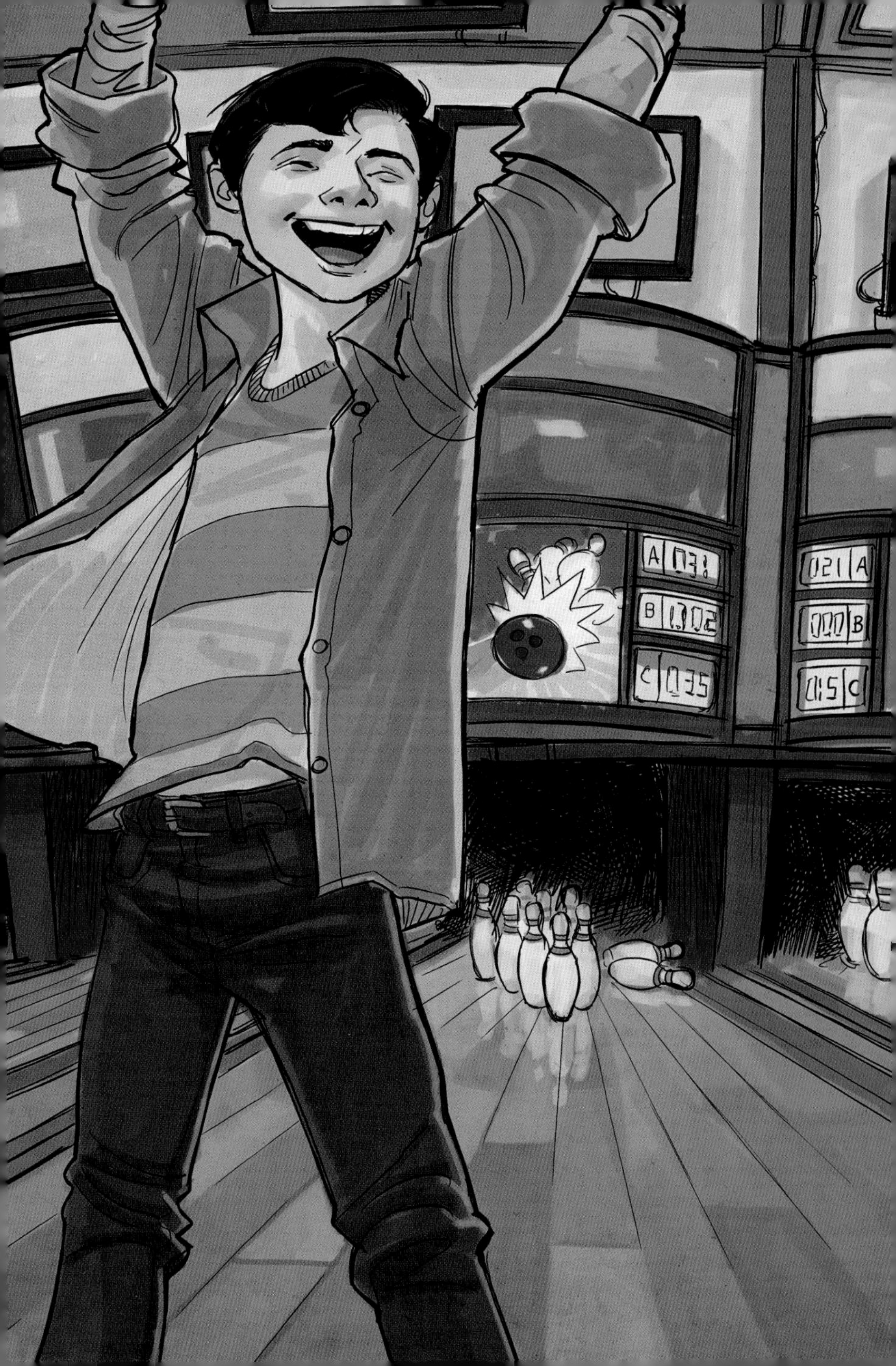

"Wow!" Sam said.

The pins rumbled around slowly. When the dust settled, only three were standing.

"Nice!" Anton said, jumping to his feet. "We are *so* going to win."

Lily sagged even more in her seat.

Then I took my turn in lane one. I couldn't throw too hard or fast, but I thought my aim was okay. I released the ball right near the middle dot at the foul line.

It rolled straight toward one side of the head pin. As it got close, though, it swerved a little and wobbled. It ended up in the gutter.

"How'd that happen?" I asked.

"Maybe it had spin on it," Sam said. "Like Mr. Spade explained."

Lily shook her head. "No way," she said. "For spin to do any good, the ball has to be going a lot faster."

"So what do you think happened?" I asked.

"You stink," Anton said, laughing. "Just like Lily the champ."

Lily rolled her eyes at him. "Only one thing could make a perfectly straight ball turn like that," she said. "There must be something wrong with the lane."

Poor Lily, I thought. *She must be really upset about this.* But to blame the lane? It seemed pretty desperate.

"So what should we do?" Gum asked.

Lily smiled. Then she snapped and ran to the front counter. We followed.

"Hey, Mr. Hayes," she said. "We'd like a new lane."

"What?" he said, looming over her from his high stool behind the counter. "Oh, hey, Lily. What's wrong with the lane you have? I thought you like lane one."

She looked at me. "It's my lucky lane," she explained. "We won on it on Saturday."

Then she turned back to Mr. Hayes. "I do like lane one, but I also use lane ten a lot," she said.

Mr. Hayes sighed. "Fine, if you're having a bad day," he said. "I'll move you over to lanes nine and ten."

"Thanks, Mr. Hayes!" Lily said. She ran over to lane one to collect her stuff.

"Wow, she knows the alley manager," I whispered to Egg.

"Then she really must bowl a lot," said Egg. "Something funny is going on."

We all got our balls and moved to lanes
nine and ten. Now it was Gum, Lily, and me
in lane ten, and Sam, Egg, and Anton at lane
nine.

Lily was excited. She grabbed her ball,
went right up to lane ten, and threw. It was a
great-looking throw. It looked just like the one
the man in lane five had thrown.

But, unlike the throw in lane five, the ball
fell right into the gutter.

"What?" Lily yelled. "I can't believe it."

"Satisfied?" Anton said snidely. "She's not
really a champ. She's just a big liar."

Lily spun and looked at Sam, then at
Gum, then at Egg, and then at me. I tried to
smile at her, but she burst into tears, covered
her face with her hands, and ran out of the
room.

CHAPTER FIVE

LILY'S PROOF

The five of us at lanes nine and ten just stood there, silently. Finally Egg tugged my sleeve.

"You should go after her," he said, pointing toward the bathrooms.

"Why me?" I said.

"Because you're a girl," he said. "She's in the girls' room."

"Oh, right," I said. I took Sam's arm. "I'll go, but you're coming with me."

The girls' bathroom at the bowling alley isn't exactly the nicest bathroom in town. There's nowhere to sit, and there's only one sink and one stall. But that made it easy to find Lily. She was hiding in the locked stall.

"Lily, it's Cat and Sam," I said.

"Go away," Lily snapped back.

"We just want to make sure you're okay," I said.

"Of course I'm not okay!" Lily shouted. "Everyone thinks I'm a liar."

Sam looked at me and shrugged.

"Lily," I said. I tried to keep my voice bright and friendly. "You have to see it from our point of view. First you told us how great you are at bowling. Then you threw three gutter balls in a row."

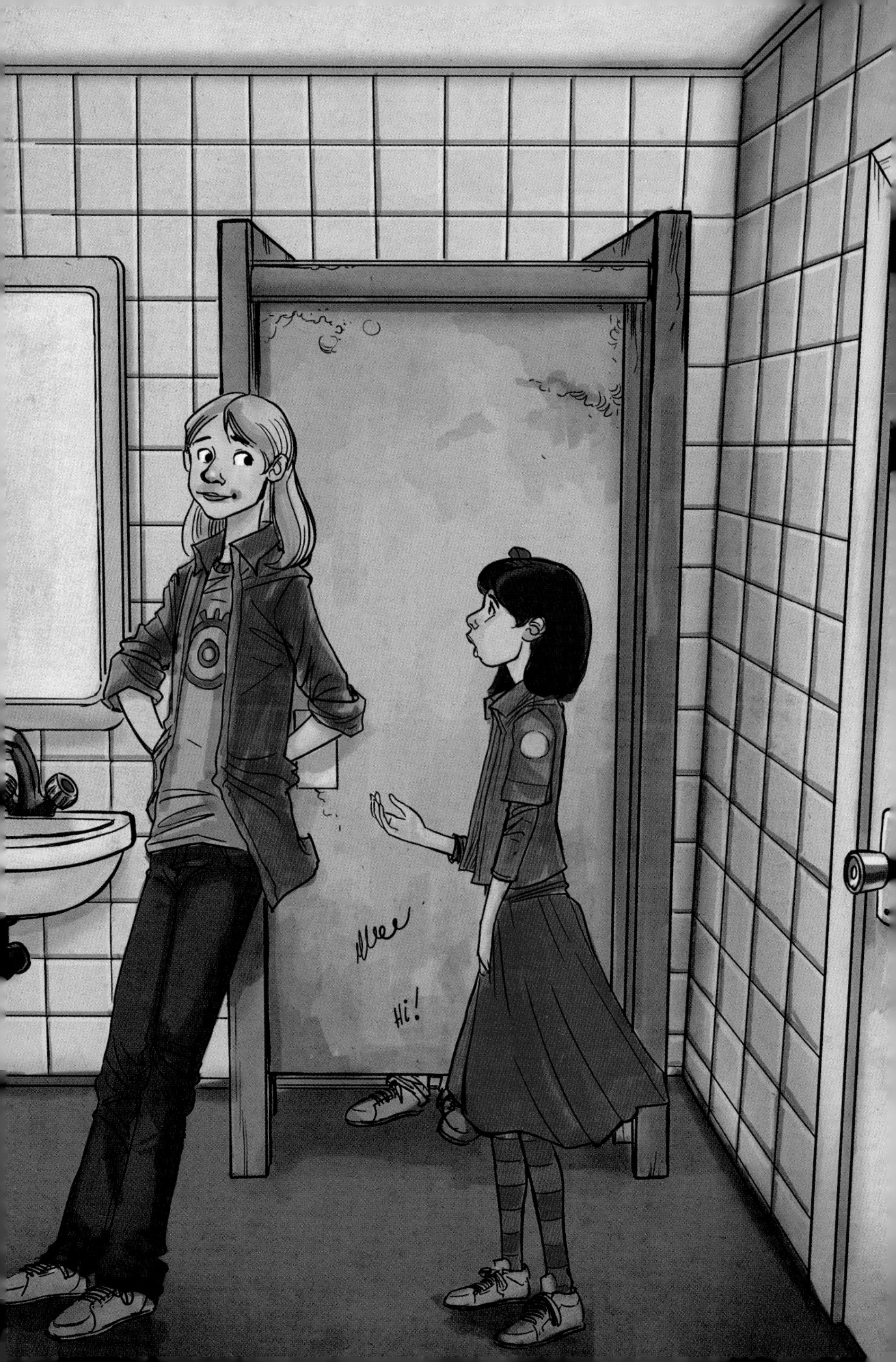
Hi!

"Five," Sam said, so I elbowed her. "Ow."

"The point is," I went on, "you have to understand that it doesn't seem like you're, well . . ."

"Any good," Sam put in.

"Sam!" I snapped.

"No," Lily said. "I get it." The lock clicked and the stall door opened. She came out, wiping her eyes. "You need proof I'm not a big liar. That makes sense." She nodded firmly. Then she took my hand. "Come on," she said, and she led us out of the bathroom, through the lobby, to the pro shop.

Inside it smelled like chemicals and cleanliness and leather. A woman behind the counter flipped through a catalog.

"Hi, Ms. Hayes," said Lily. "I just came to show my friends the photo from Saturday."

"Hi, Lily," the woman said. "We already framed it and hung it up." She nodded to the wall behind us.

There, among hundreds of photos of bowling teams from the last fifty years, was a picture of man and a girl. He held a big trophy, and she held a little sign that said: "James and Lily McDonald, Father-Daughter League Champs."

"There's your proof," Lily said. She crossed her arms and stared at Sam.

"That's pretty great proof," Sam said. "I'm sorry."

"Me too," I said.

"Thank you," said Lily. We headed back toward lanes nine and ten.

As we walked, I asked, "So what's going on today? Is it just your arm?"

"Well," Lily said, her face bright red, "to be honest, my arm feels fine. I should be having a great day."

"Well, we already tried changing lanes," I said. "Why don't you try a different ball?"

"Yeah!" said Sam as we stepped up to the lane. She glared at Anton. "I bet that stinker did something to yours. He was really irritated that you brought your own."

Lily shrugged. "Would he really do that?" she asked.

Gum laughed and said, "You don't know him too well, do you?"

CHAPTER SIX

THE SUSPECTS

"Why would I mess with her ball?" Anton asked. Lily, my friends, and I stood in a half circle around him so he couldn't run off for a soda or another pretzel.

"You said yourself it wasn't fair," Gum pointed out.

"Please," Anton said, rolling his eyes. "Sure, I said that. But that was before I saw her bowl. She obviously stinks. I'm happy to just sit back and watch her fail. I didn't touch her ball."

"Prove it," Lily said.

"I can't," Anton said. "But you can't prove I did. So . . ."

With that, he shoved between me and Lily and walked off. "Time for a slushee," he said.

"He's got us there," Sam said. "The burden of proof rests with us, not him."

"Right," I said. "He's innocent until proven guilty."

"But we'll still keep an eye on him," Sam added.

"We will?" Gum said. "Huh. Usually I'm the only one who blames Anton."

"It's useless," said Lily. "Maybe I should just call it a day. I'm ruining the game for everyone." She walked away by herself.

"So now what?" Egg asked. "Is this a real mystery now? Are we on a case?"

Sam nodded toward the concession stand and started to lead us over there so we could talk in private. Anton was just heading back to our lanes with his drink.

"Where are you dorks going?" he asked. "Are we ever going to finish this game?"

"We'll be there in a minute," growled Gum. "And you better hope we don't find anything that proves you are the cause of Lily's bad day."

Anton huffed and walked off. The four of us huddled together.

"So?" Egg repeated. "Are we on the case?"

I looked at Lily. She sure seemed sad. "Yes," I said. "We have to figure this out for Lily."

"Okay," Sam said. "Who are our suspects?"

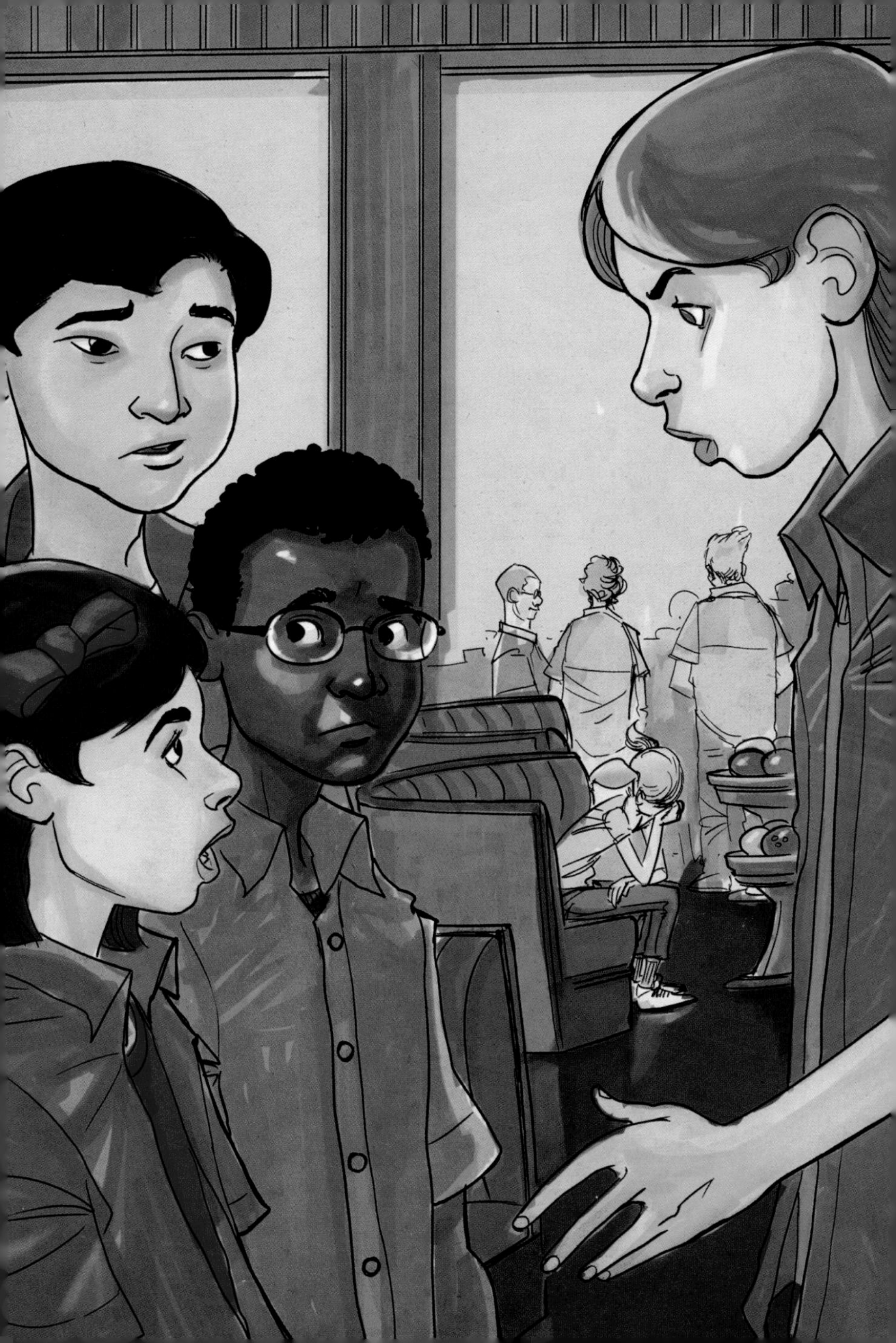

"So far?" Gum said. "Just Anton."

"And Lily," Sam pointed out.

"What?" I asked, confused. "Why would Lily mess up her own ball?"

Sam shrugged. "Who knows?" she said. "We don't even know if the ball is the problem. We do know that Lily has had access to the ball. No one else has."

"True," Gum said. "But still."

"Maybe her dad pressures her to bowl," Egg said. "Maybe she's sick of the pressure, and this is her way of escaping her overbearing father!"

Gum, Sam, and I looked at him. "It's possible," Egg said.

"What about her?" Sam said. She pointed back toward lane ten.

Lily was still there, slumped in her seat, and Anton was there, slurping his drink. But there another girl too, on a bench just off to the side. She was watching Lily. And she was smiling.

"That girl looks awfully happy that Lily is sad, doesn't she?" Sam said. "Let's go have a chat with her."

Everyone agreed that since I was the friendliest of our group, I should talk to the girl on my own. "Hi," I said, walking up to her. "I'm Cat."

"Um, hi," the girl said.

"You're not in our class," I said. "Are you on a field trip too?"

"No," the girl said. "My school is closed today, for parent-teacher conferences. So I'm bowling with my dad."

She pointed at lane five. "That's him, over there," she said.

"Oh," I said. "He's an expert bowler! Our teacher showed us how he throws the ball right along the edge and then it curves into the pins just the right way."

"Yeah," the girl said. "He's great. I'm pretty good too."

"Is that right?" I asked.

The girl nodded and went back to watching Lily sulk. "She doesn't look very good, though," she said. "I've been watching her bowl."

"What do you know about Lily?" I said.

"I know that she and her dad beat me and my dad in the championship on Saturday," the girl said. "Honestly, I'm glad she's having a bad day."

"Jealous?" I asked. I admit, she was making me angry.

"Of course I am," said the girl as she stood up. "I don't like to lose. But I'll definitely beat her score today."

Then she stomped off back to lane five.

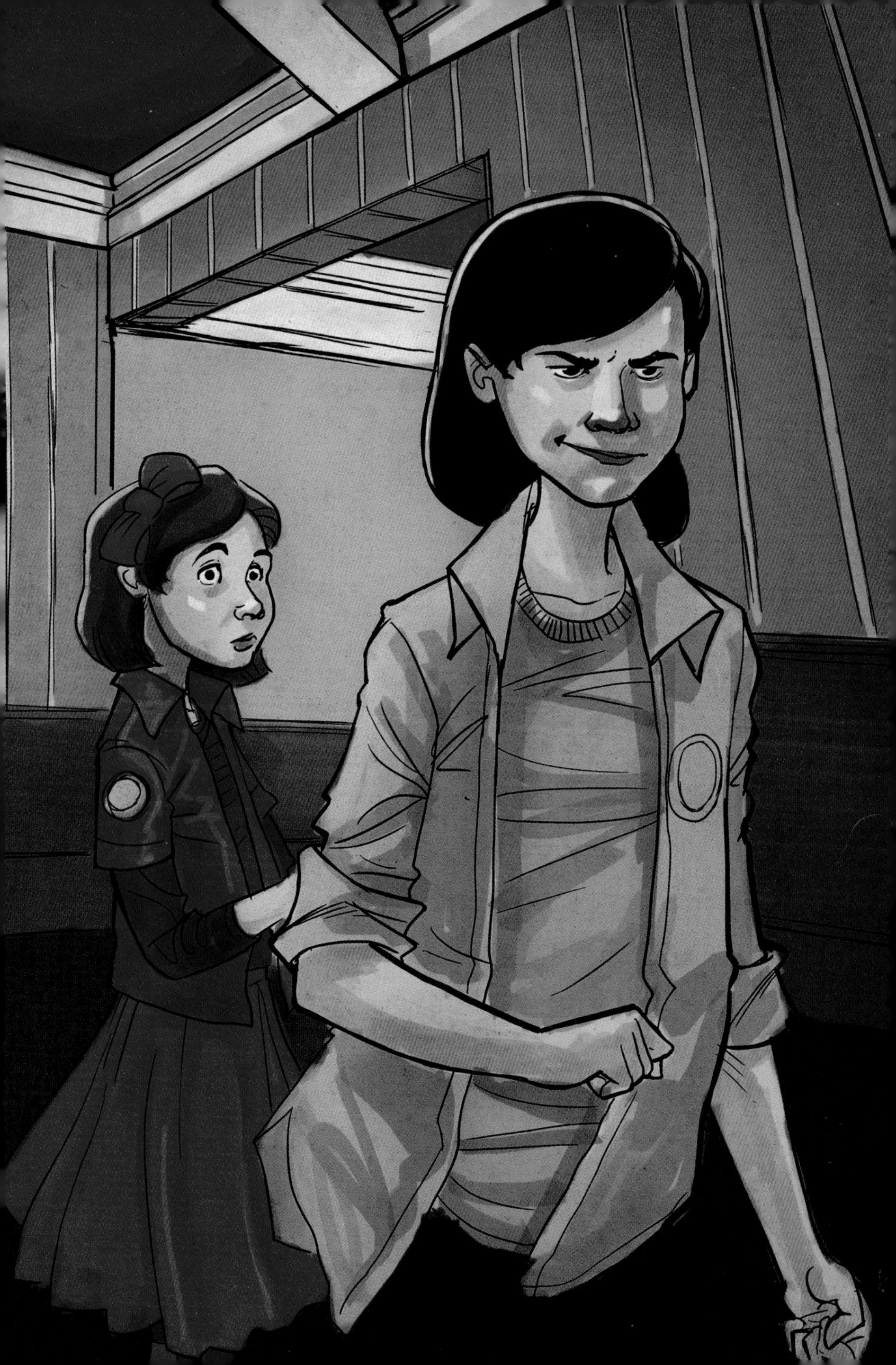

"That makes three suspects," Sam said. She pulled her notebook out of her pocket and made some notes.

"You're still counting Lily?" I asked. "Look at her. She's miserable."

Gum nodded. "It's true, Sam," he said. "I don't think she's lying, and I don't think she sabotaged her own ball."

"I know, I know," Sam said. "But right now she's the only person with the opportunity, and that's one thing the suspect always needs. That and motive."

"Well, she has no motive," I said.

"That we know of," Egg pointed out. I glared at him. "Well, it's true," he said.

"Then there's only one thing we can do," Gum said. "Figure out when someone else had an opportunity to mess with Lily."

Egg lifted his camera. He nearly always has it around his neck, and today was no different. He had snapped a few photos of our lanes, with Anton looking smug and Lily looking miserable.

"Cameras!" Sam said, snapping her fingers. She looked at the ceiling, and then at the walls. "Egg, you're a genius."

"I am?" Egg asked.

"Come on, guys," Sam said. Then she ran toward a door marked "Office."

"I'm sorry, kids," said a man in a blue uniform in the office. He shook his head. "I can't just show the security footage to anyone."

Behind him were four monitors. Each one showed black-and-white footage of different spots in the bowling alley. From this spot, the security guard could watch every spot in the bowling alley — except for the bathrooms.

"But it's very important," Sam said. "We're trying to solve a crime."

"A crime?" he said. He narrowed his eyes. "No one told me about any crime."

"Well," I said, "it might not actually be a crime."

I told him about the bad morning Lily was having.

"Lily McDonald?" the security guard said. "Why didn't you say so? I'd do just about anything for Lily."

"Wow," I said. "Everyone loves her down here, don't they?"

The security guard nodded and smiled. "Gather 'round, kids," he said. "Let's watch some footage."

* * *

We watched clip after clip of video from the cameras. The security guard was able to follow every movement of Lily's ball and bag from the moment we walked into the building up until that very second.

No one but Lily ever touched it.

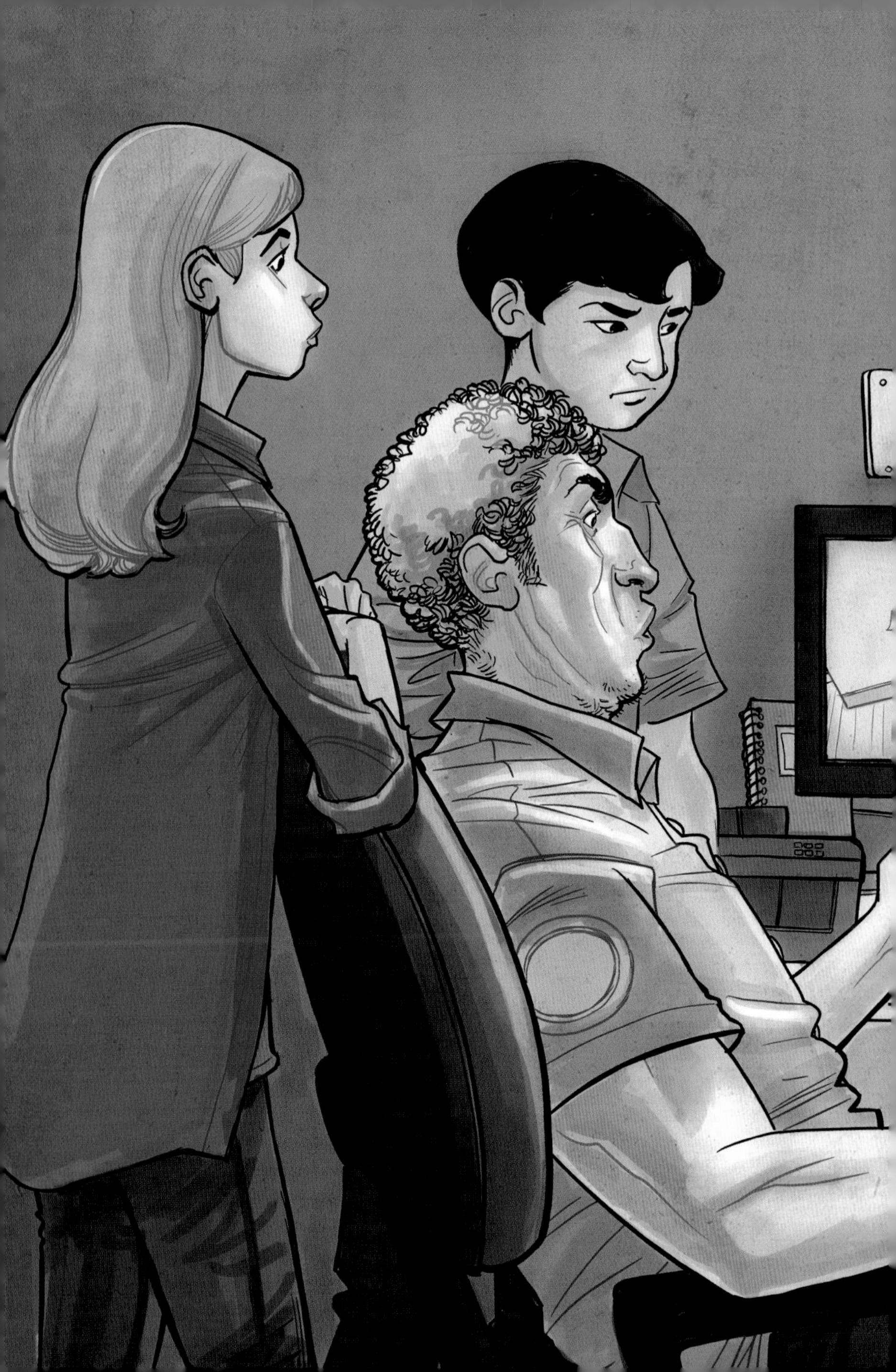

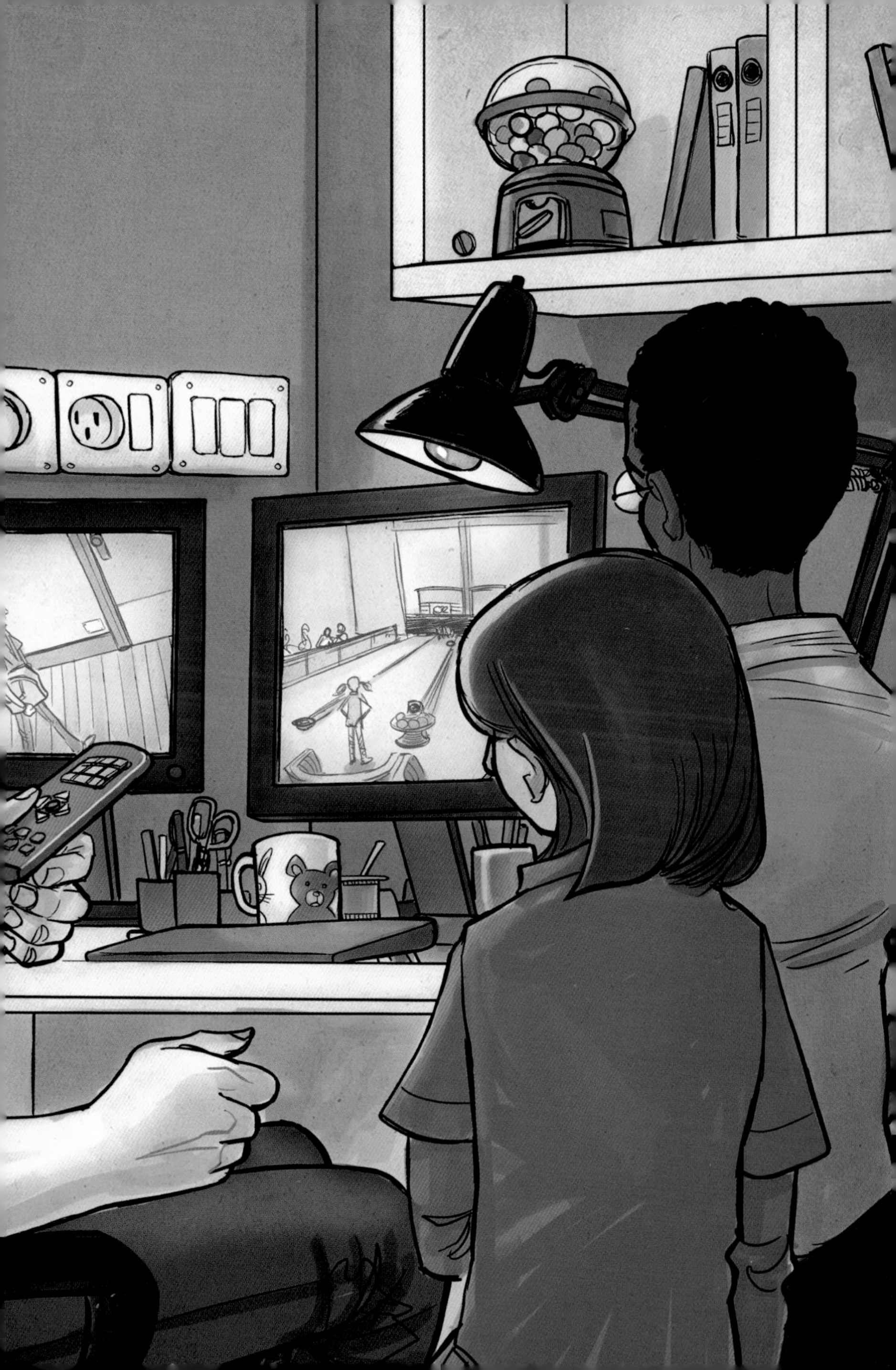

"Sorry, kids," the guard said. He rubbed his head in frustration. "I really wish I could've helped. But no one messed with Lily's ball. At least not today."

"Not in this building today," Gum pointed out in a whisper as we left the office. "But that doesn't rule out the bus."

Sam smiled. "So Anton is still a prime suspect," she said. "We better talk to Lily."

CHAPTER NINE

STRIKES AT LAST

"I honestly can't remember," Lily said when we asked her about the bus ride. "I think I had my bag at my feet for the whole bus ride, but why do you want to know?"

"We suspect sabotage," Sam said. She paced in front of the bench where Lily and I were sitting.

"Sabotage?" said Lily, alarmed.

"Well, we know Anton wasn't happy that you brought your own ball," Sam said.

"Hey!" Anton said from lane nine's bench.

"And we know Anton is a dirty rotten meanie," Gum said.

"I can hear you, you know," Anton said. He crossed his arms and sneered at us.

"It's possible that Anton did something to your ball," I said quietly, trying to make sure Anton wouldn't overhear this time.

Lily shook her head. "No," she said. "I had it with me the whole time. Besides," she added, leaning over to show me, "it locks. See?"

A little, golden padlock held the bag's zipper closed. There was no way anyone could have gotten in there without the little key, which was in Lily's pocket.

Gum and Sam leaned back on lane ten's scorekeeper table. Egg sat down near the foul line. We all four sighed.

"Guys, thanks a lot for trying," Lily says. "This is no mystery, though. I'm just having a very bad day."

She picked up her ball from the carousel. Since Egg was blocking lane ten, she went over to lane nine.

"Hey, use your own lane!" Anton protested.

"Oh, you shush," I said. Sometimes Anton is just too much even for me.

"Let me demonstrate how bad my day is," Lily said. And she pulled back and threw her ball down lane nine.

It flew along the edge, just like last time, but this time it didn't slip into the gutter. It turned before the pins and crashed with a boom.

"Strike!" I shouted.

"What?" Anton said. "I — I don't believe it."

Lily's jaw hung open. "I don't either," she said.

"Do that again!" Gum said. He grabbed her ball as it came up the return and handed it to her.

"Um, okay," Lily said. And she did! Another perfect throw, and another strike.

We cheered. Anton called over our hoorays, "I hope you know you just bowled two strikes in a row in my team's lane!"

Lily stuck her tongue out at him. Then she grabbed her ball and hurried to lane ten. She threw.

Gutter ball.

"Ha, ha!" Anton said, but we didn't care. The mystery was nearly solved. It had to be the lane.

"I think we better go check with our new friend in the office," Sam said. "If lane ten is the problem —"

"And lane one," Gum pointed out.

Sam nodded. "Then we need to figure out why," she said. And we headed to the office.

BAD LUCK?

An hour later, Sam slumped in the chair in front of the security monitors. "I just don't get it," she said. "We watched so much footage of lanes one and ten. And no one did a thing to them."

The security guard stood behind Sam with his hands on his hips. "Sorry, kids," he said. "Are you sure it's not just bad luck?"

"Bad luck?" I said. "Click over to lane nine and see for yourself."

He did, and there was a black-and-white video of Lily, throwing strike after strike, with Anton watching and sulking.

The security smiled. "That's why she's the champ!" he said. Then the phone rang.

"Hello?" he said. "Oh, yes, Mr. Hayes. I'll be right there." He grabbed a set of keys from the desk. "Sorry, kids," he said. "Time to lock up the office. I have to go let a delivery man in the side door."

We shuffled out, and he grabbed a big, yellow raincoat from the behind the door. "It's a real pain to get deliveries on a rainy day like this," the security guard said, pulling on the raincoat. "Third day in a row. Ugh!"

He led us back to the main part of the alley and then disappeared out the front door. Lightning cracked and thunder exploded across the gray mid-morning sky.

As I watched him go, I remembered a time when my dad left a window open in our house during a downpour. Water got in and the wood floor got wet. A small section of the floor is bumpy and warped to this day.

"We need to talk to Mr. Hayes," I said. I grabbed Sam by the hand and off we ran to find him.

THE DISCOVERY

Mr. Hayes was on his big stool behind the front counter. He was scribbling with a pencil and punching a calculator. He didn't seem happy.

"Mr. Hayes?" I said.

"What is it?" he snapped. "Can't you see I'm busy?"

"Sorry, sir," I said. "I just thought you'd like to know that lanes one and ten are warped."

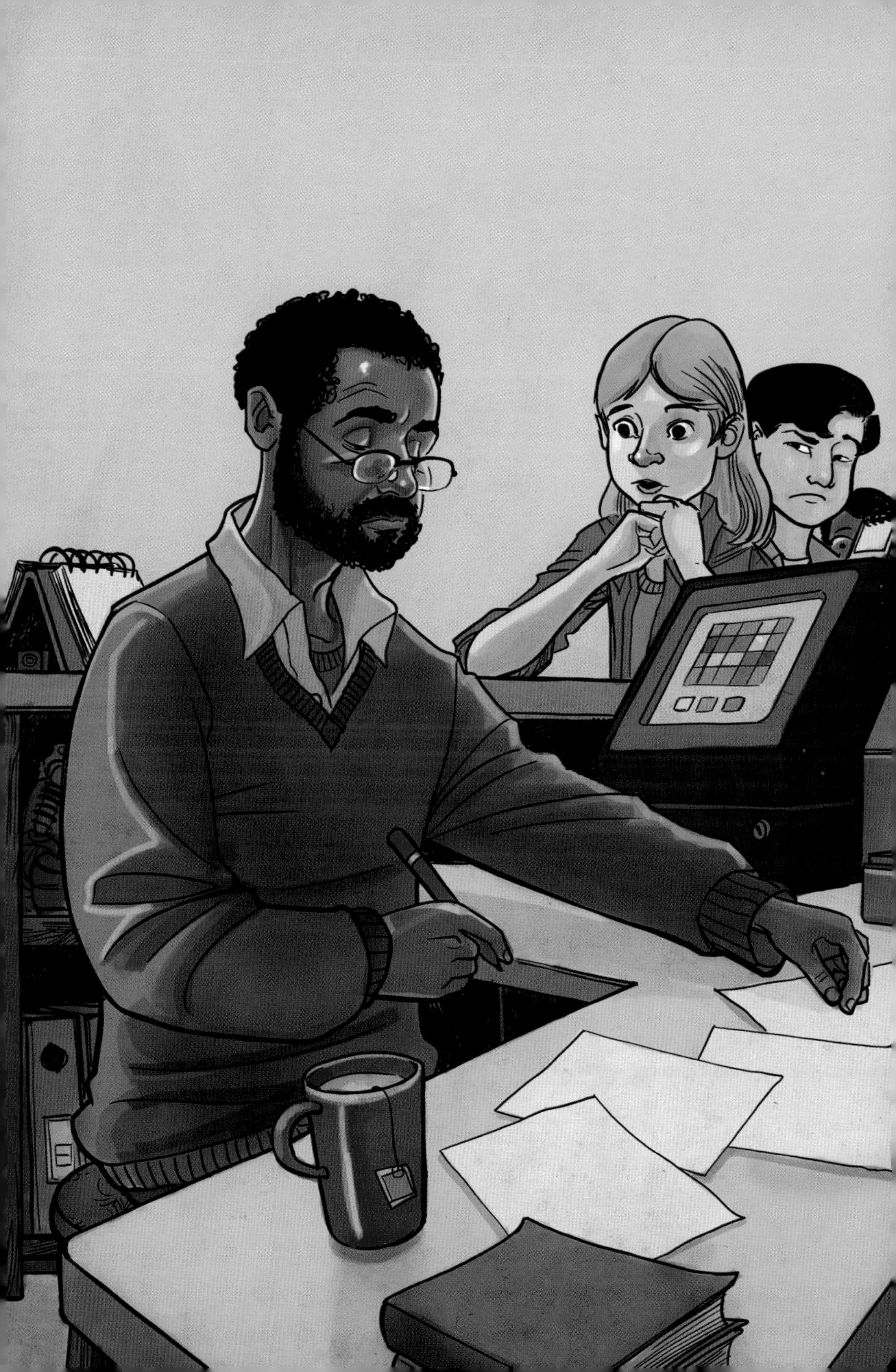

That got his attention.
"What!?" he said.

"It's true," Egg put in. "One girl has bowled nothing but gutter balls all morning."

"Ha," Mr. Hayes said, looking back at his paperwork. "She probably needs more practice, not new lanes."

Sam smiled. "What would you say if I told you that the bowler was Lily McDonald?" she asked.

Mr. Hayes looked up sharply. "Nonsense!" he said. "Lily's the finest young bowler I've ever known, and that's saying something."

"See for yourself," said Gum. He shouted across the room. "Hey, Lily. Try it on lane ten!"

She looked over and nodded. Then she strolled to lane ten, approached, and released. The ball zoomed down the right side of the lane.

Mr. Hayes watched, smiling and nodding. "A perfect throw," he said.

But then the ball wobbled and slipped into the gutter.

"What?!" Mr. Hayes yelled. He hopped down from his stool and ran to lane ten.

We stood at the end of the lane and watched as he carefully walked along the gutter. Near the pins, he got down on his knees and ran his hand over the wood. His face went pale.

"Lane one is the same way," I said when Mr. Hayes came back from his inspection.

Mr. Hayes shook his head. "I can't understand it," he said. "The lanes were fine for the Father-Daughter Championship on Saturday."

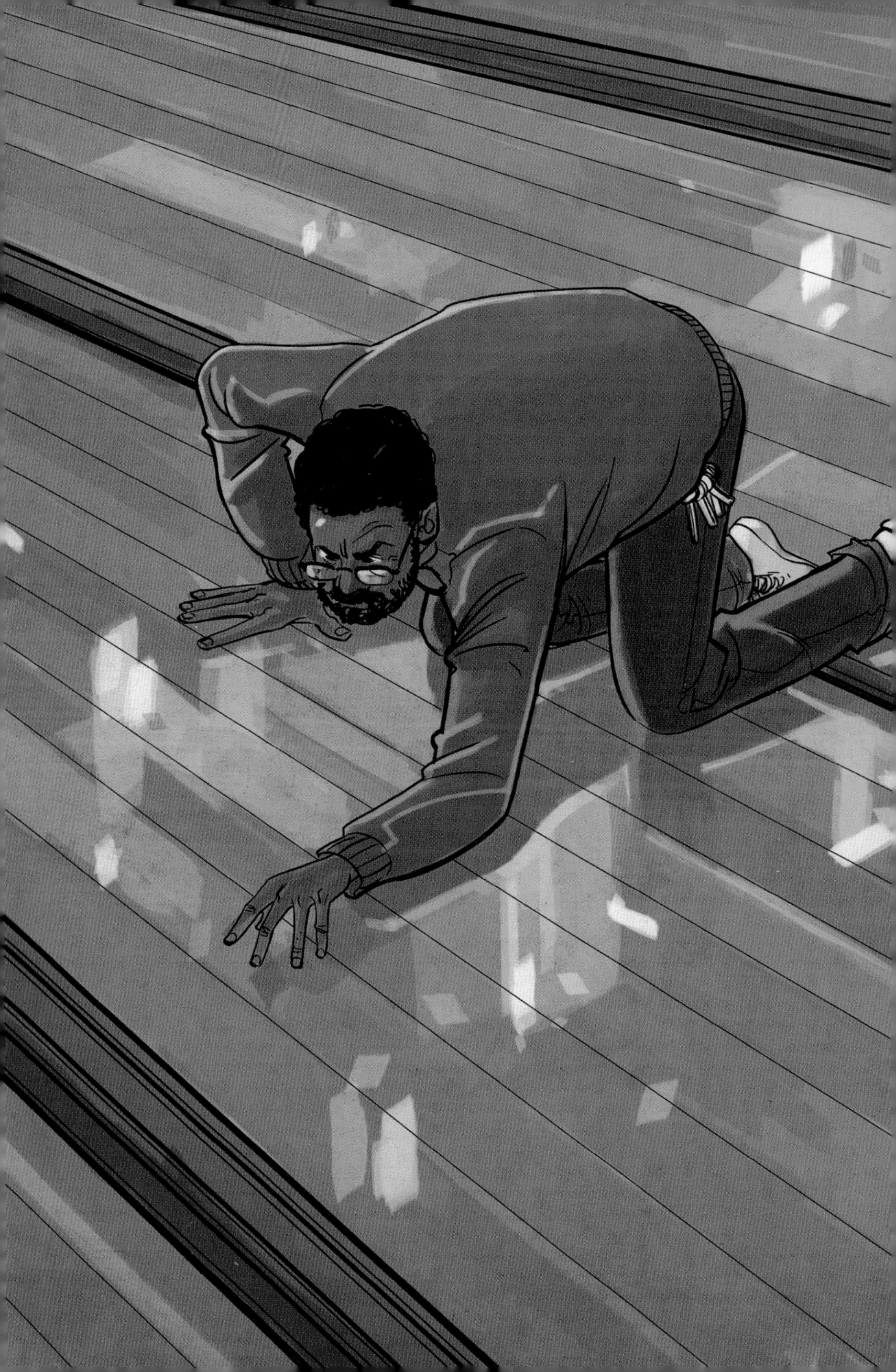

"That was before the rain," I pointed out. "Too much moisture can ruin wood."

I hurried down the gutter, just like Mr. Hayes had.

"Hey, you can't go down there," Mr. Hayes called after me, but I wasn't going far. About halfway down the lane, I knelt and pushed down on the dark-blue carpeting along the outside wall. A puddle formed around my hand.

"Oh, my," Mr. Hayes said. "That's not good." He sighed. "I guess I'd better call a repairman and the carpet cleaners." He sat down next to Anton and pulled out his phone.

I hurried back to my friends. "So that solves this one, I guess," I said.

Sam shrugged. "No crook," she said. "How boring."

"Yeah," said Gum. "It was just the dumb, old rain."

Mr. Hayes clicked off his phone and stood up with a grunt.

"Well, this is going to get expensive," he said, looking out over the warped lane ten. "I just can't figure it out, though."

"Can't figure what out?" I asked.

"Sure, it's been raining," he said, "but I don't get why the dehumidifier didn't clear the air." He headed back to the front desk, shaking his head.

Sam's face suddenly lit up. "Guys," she said in her secret crime-busting voice, "this mystery isn't over yet."

"If you say so," I said. I was confused, but after a few times solving crimes with Sam, I've learned to trust her.

Egg, Gum, Lily, and I ran after Sam as she headed for the office again. The door was locked.

"Drat," Sam said. "Where is —"

"You kids looking for me?" said the guard.

He walked over to us, still shaking out his raincoat. "It's still raining cats and dogs out there."

"We need another look at that footage, sir," Sam said. "But this time, we won't be looking at the lanes."

SABOTAGE

After finding what she needed and explaining everything to us, Sam stood up from the security guard's chair.

"Just a minute, Sam," the guard said.

"Yeah?" she said.

"Lily may be the best bowler in your school," he said, "but you're the best detective. If you ever need a summer job, come find me. I'll have something for you to do in security around here."

Sam beamed. "Thanks," she said. "Right now, we have a crook to grab."

He saluted her, and the five of us ran to lane five.

"There she is," Lily said. "I should have known."

She pointed at the girl we'd spoken to earlier — the same girl Lily had beaten in the Father-Daughter Championship on Saturday.

Lily got right in her face. "Hello, Annie," she said. "Admit what you did."

The girl closed her eyes and crossed her arms. "I don't know what you're talking about," she said, smiling.

Her father, the expert bowler, put down his ball and came over. "What's going on here?" he asked.

Mr. Spade saw the commotion, too. He jogged over from lane three. "What's the problem?" he asked. "Kids, why are you bothering these people?"

"We'll show you, Mr. Spade," said Sam. She turned and faced the office and put her hands around her mouth like a bullhorn. "Okay, now! Play it now, Chuck!"

The lights in the bowling alley flickered and went dim. Then all the scorekeeping screens hanging over the lanes flashed bright white.

"Hey, what happened to the scores?" Anton shouted.

The TVs all flicked back on. But now, instead of colorful bowling scores, they showed black-and-white surveillance video.

The video wasn't of any of the lanes, and it wasn't of Lily's ball bag. It was of a room in the basement of the bowling alley.

There were Annie and her father, skulking through the room with flashlights. Annie's father carried a big wrench.

"What's the meaning of this?" Mr. Hayes shouted. He jumped up from his stool and ran to lane five.

As we watched, the fuzzy figures on the screen approached a big piece of equipment in the center of the big basement room.

"My dehumidifier!" Mr. Hayes said.

Then, on the screens, Annie's father leaned down behind the appliance and pulled out a heavy-looking cord. The appliance stopped shimmying and shaking. He'd turned it off.

"There you have it," Sam said. "Proof positive: sabotage."

Mr. Hayes stepped up to Annie and her father. "What do you have to say for yourselves?" he asked.

We decided to give them some space to deal with the issue. "And to think they nearly got away with it," Sam said.

"I guess Annie's a pretty sore loser," Lily said, shrugging. Then she walked off to gather her things.

As she strolled away, I couldn't help but notice the expression on her face. Lily McDonald was finally smiling.

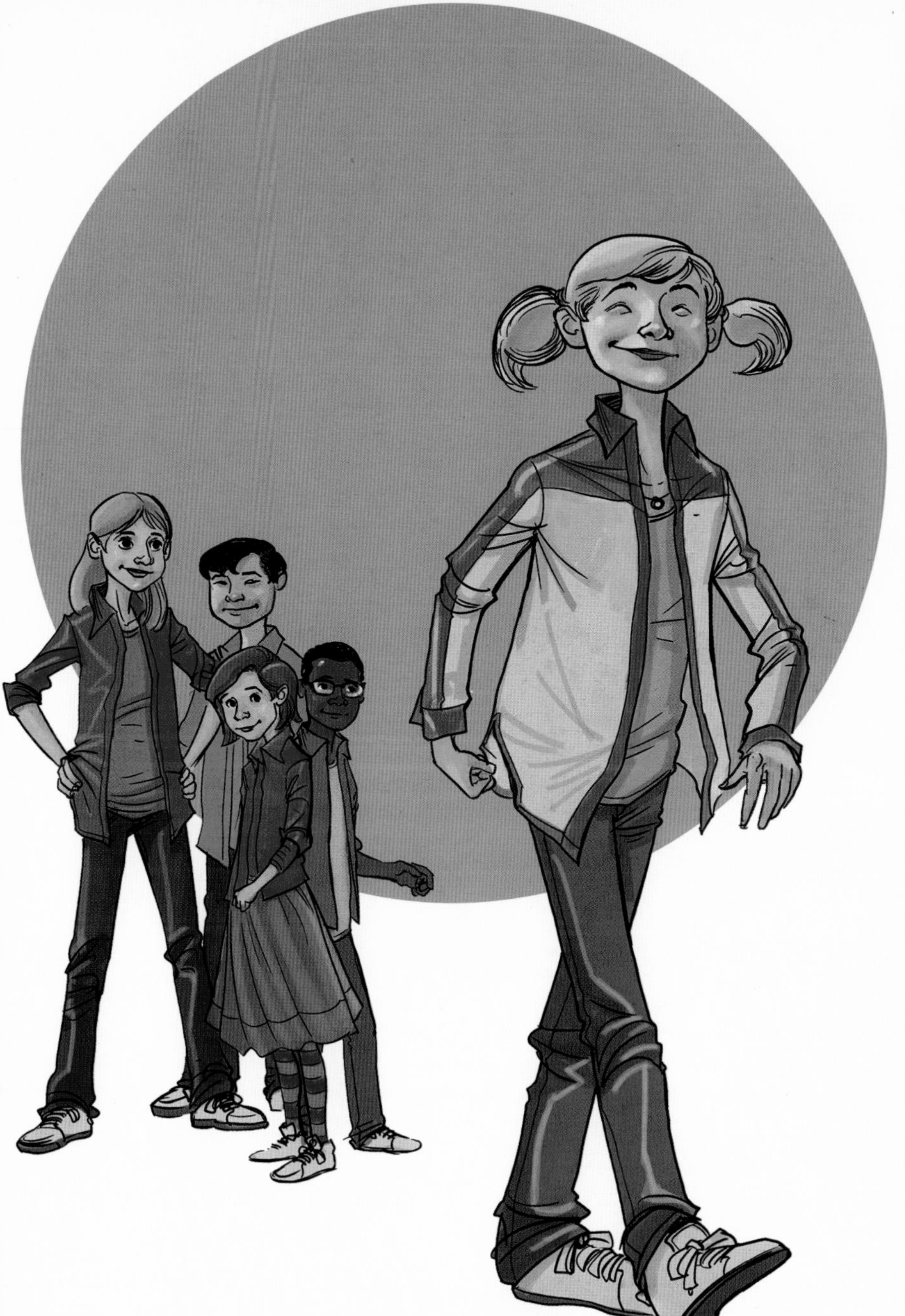

literary news

MYSTERIOUS WRITER REVEALED!

Steve Brezenoff lives in Minneapolis, Minnesota, with his wife, Beth and their son, Sam. Besides writing books, he enjoys playing video games, riding his bicycle, and helping middle-school students work on their writing skills. Steve's ideas almost always come to him in his dreams, so he does his best writing in his pajamas.

arts & entertainment

ARTIST IS KEY TO SOLVING MYSTERY, SAY POLICE

Marcos Calo lives happily in A Coruña, Spain, with his wife, Patricia (who is also an illustrator), and their daughter, Claudia. When Marcos and Patricia aren't drawing, they like to go on long walks by the sea. They also watch a lot of films and eat Nutella sandwiches. Yum!

A Detective's Dictionary

dehumidifier (dee-hyoo-MID-uh-fye-er)–a machine that removes moisture from the air

demonstrate (DEM-uhn-strate)–to show other people how to do something

desperate (DESS-pur-it)–willing to do anything to change your situation

innocent (IN-uh-suhnt)–not guilty

insisted (in-SIST-id)–demanded firmly

inspection (in-SPEK-shuhn)–the act of looking at something carefully

lounging (LOUNJ-ing)–sitting in a lazy way

motive (MOH-tiv)–a reason for doing something

physics (FIZ-iks)–the science that deals with matter and energy. It includes the study of light, heat, sound, electricity, motion, and force.

sabotage (SAB-uh-tahzh)–the deliberate damage or destruction of property

surveillance (ser-VEY-luhns)–close watch

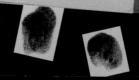

Cat Duran

6th Grade

Bowling

Bowling has been around for longer than even those smelly shoes at the bowling alley. No one knows for sure, but some historians think ancient Egyptians enjoyed a version of the game as early as 3200 BC.

There were many different versions of early bowling. People still play a crazy version in Edinburgh, Scotland. It uses a ball without any finger holes. The bowler swings the ball between his or her legs, throwing it toward the pins. Then the bowler flops onto the lane, lying on the stomach!

Dutch, English, and German immigrants all brought their versions of bowling to America.

In 1841, however, a law was passed in Connecticut that made it illegal to run "ninepin lanes." This was probably because people made bets over bowling, and gambling was illegal.

Finally, in 1895, a New York restaurant owner named Joe Thum led area bowling clubs in forming the American Bowling Congress. That meant that standard rules could be made. The group also began holding national bowling competitions.

Today, bowling is found in more than 90 countries worldwide. It is also a very popular activity for birthday parties and field trips!

Cat, Very nice work. I wonder what kind of physics is involved in that Scottish version of bowling. – Mr. S.

FURTHER INVESTIGATIONS

CASE #FTM18CDSBT

1. Have you ever been bowling? What was the hardest part? What was the most fun?

2. Did you have any other suspects in this mystery? Who were they? Talk about your reasons.

3. Do you think field trips are an important part of school? Why or why not?

IN YOUR OWN DETECTIVE'S NOTEBOOK . . .

1. When she didn't bowl well, Lily's day did not go as well as expected. Have you ever had a disappointing day? Write about it.

2. Think of the most recent field trip you went on. Where did you go? Write about it.

3. This book is a mystery story. Write your own mystery story!

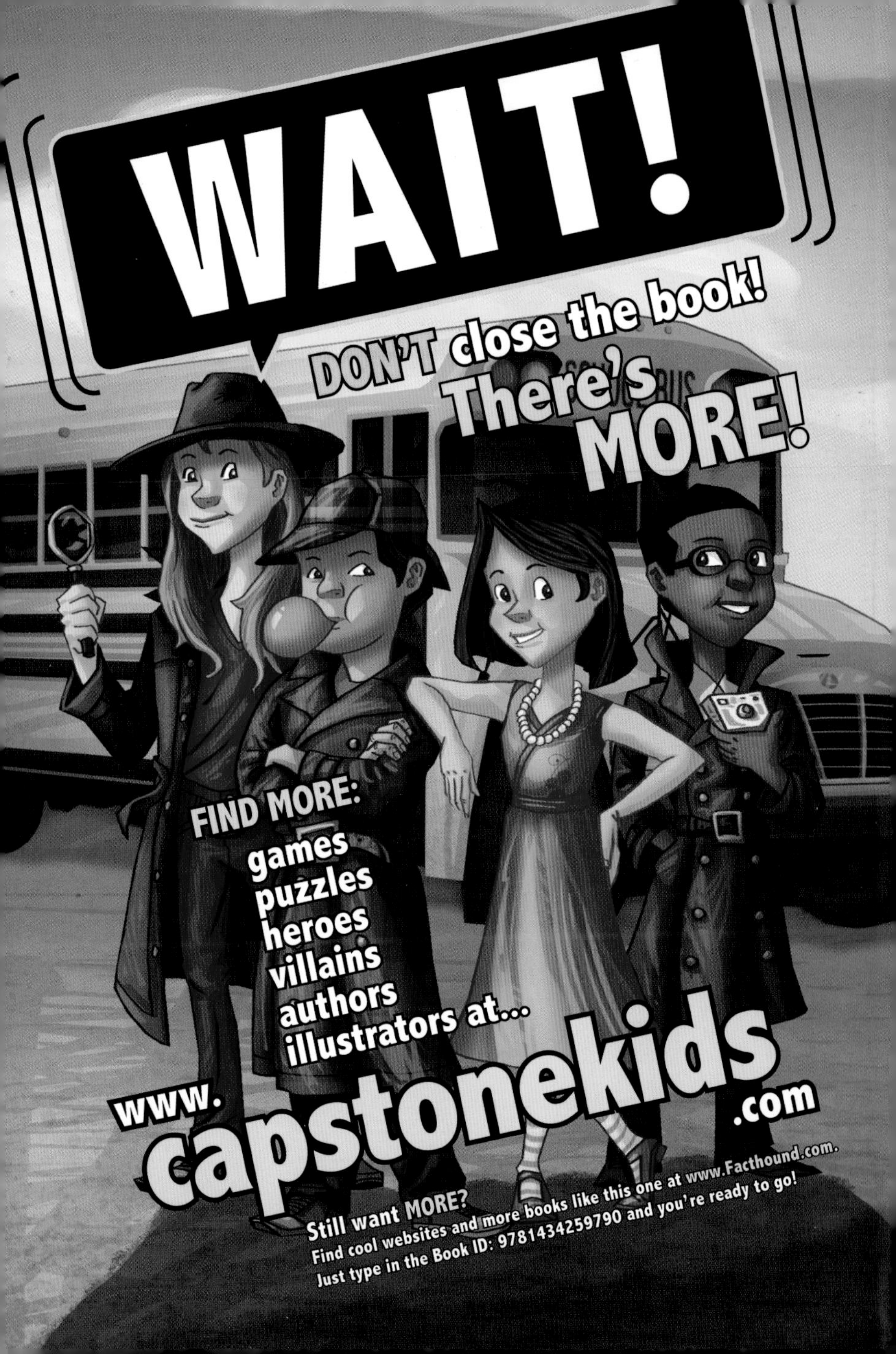
WAIT!
DON'T close the book!
There's MORE!
FIND MORE:
games
puzzles
heroes
villains
authors
illustrators at...
www.
capstonekids
.com
Still want MORE?
Find cool websites and more books like this one at www.Facthound.com.
Just type in the Book ID: 9781434259790 and you're ready to go!

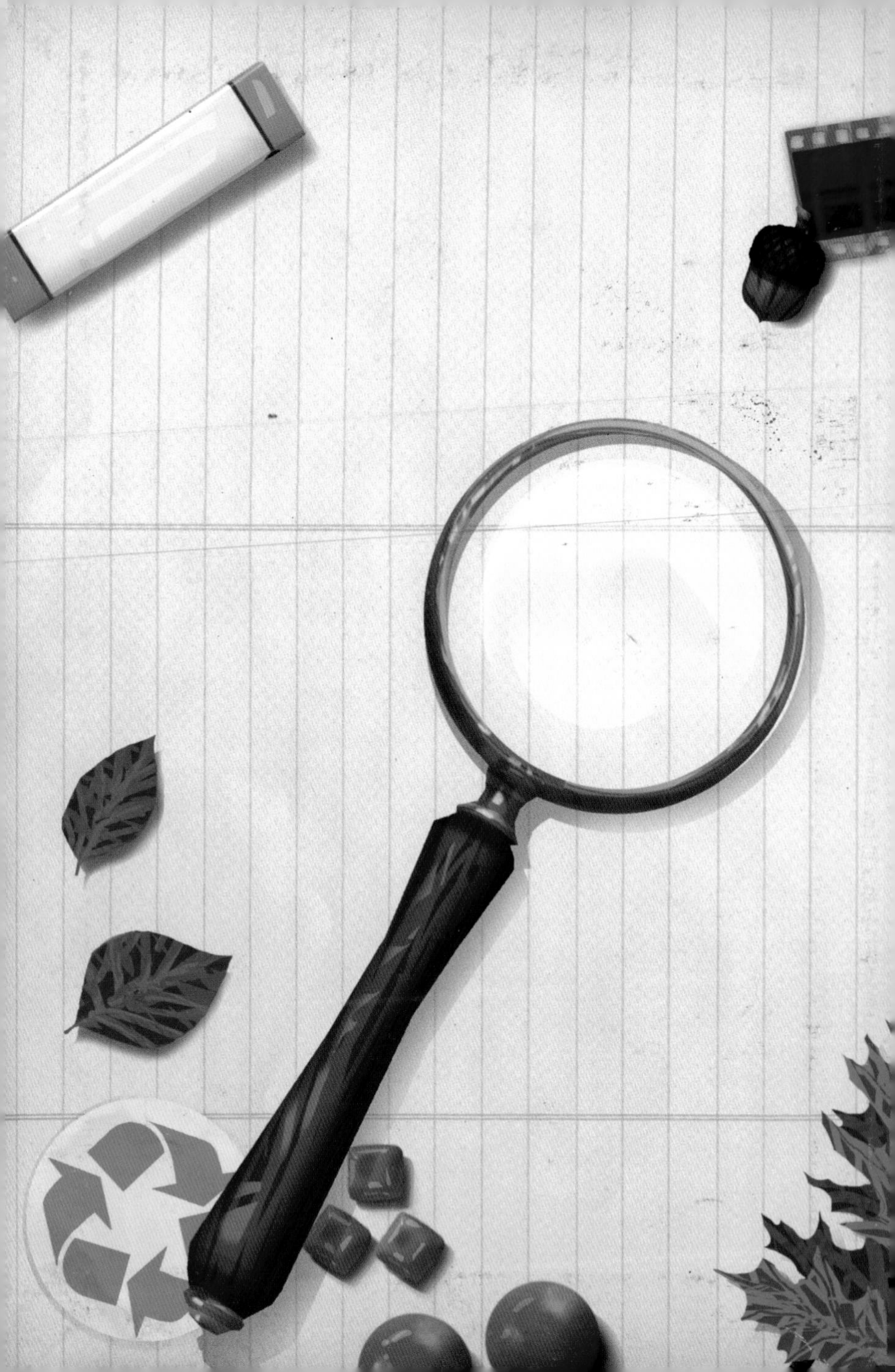